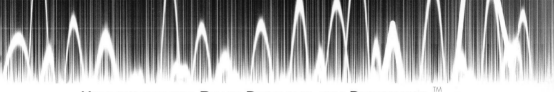

UNDERSTANDING BRAIN DISEASES AND DISORDERS™

BRAIN INJURIES

AUBREY STIMOLA

ROSEN
PUBLISHING®

New York

Published in 2012 by The Rosen Publishing Group, Inc.
29 East 21st Street, New York, NY 10010

Library of Congress Cataloging-in-Publication Data

Stimola, Aubrey.
Brain injuries/Aubrey Stimola.—1st ed.
     p. cm.—(Understanding brain diseases and disorders)
Includes bibliographical references and index.
ISBN 978-1-4488-5543-8 (lib. bdg.)
1. Brain—Wounds and injuries—Juvenile literature. I. Title.
RD594.S75 2012
617.4'81044—dc23

2011015277

Manufactured in China

CPSIA Compliance Information: Batch #W12YA: For further information, contact Rosen Publishing, New York, New York, at
1-800-237-9932.

CONTENTS

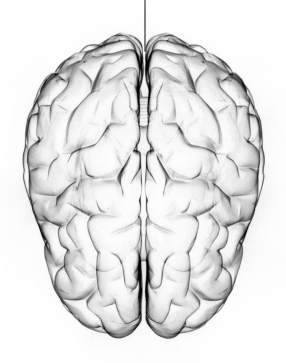

Introduction

T he brain is an amazing organ. Seated within the protective case of the skull, the brain is the body's control center, a central computer that coordinates, controls, and regulates emotion, behavior, thinking, learning, remembering, dreaming, and communicating. It shapes our personalities and dreams and makes us human. It is also responsible for some of the most basic body functions necessary to sustain life, such as the regulation of breathing, heart rate, blood pressure, and body temperature. If these functions are not strictly regulated by the brain, the human body cannot survive.

Just as other parts of the body are vulnerable to injury, as in breaking a bone or cutting the skin, the brain, too, can be injured and its functions disrupted as a result. Brain injury can result in loss of specific, localized functions, such as vision, use of a specific limb, or the ability to speak or understand the speech of others. Brain injury can also result in loss of more global functions such as learning, communication with others, and control of movement and other behavior.

Some people with permanent injury to the brain adapt to the specific loss of function and learn to live differently to compensate. In more severe cases, injury to the brain can result in an inability to live independently or without the use of machines. In the most extreme cases, brain injury can result in death.

The effects of a specific brain injury depend on the location of the injury and how severe it is. This book will look briefly at the basic structure and function of the most important parts of the brain and will explore the effects of different types of injury to these areas. Additionally, more general forms of brain injury will be explored. Later chapters will touch upon some treatments, new research, and prevention of some types of brain injury.

In order to discuss injury to the brain and the loss of specific functions that can result from such injuries, we must first understand the basic structure of the brain and roles played by its different parts and areas. The study of the brain is part of a field of science called neurobiology. In the last few decades, scientists' understanding of the brain and nervous system has grown rapidly and research is ongoing. This has opened doors to a better understanding of the nature of various types of brain injury and how they might be prevented, treated, or even cured. Despite the advancements made in the neurobiology field, there is still much we do not know about the brain and much more for scientists to discover.

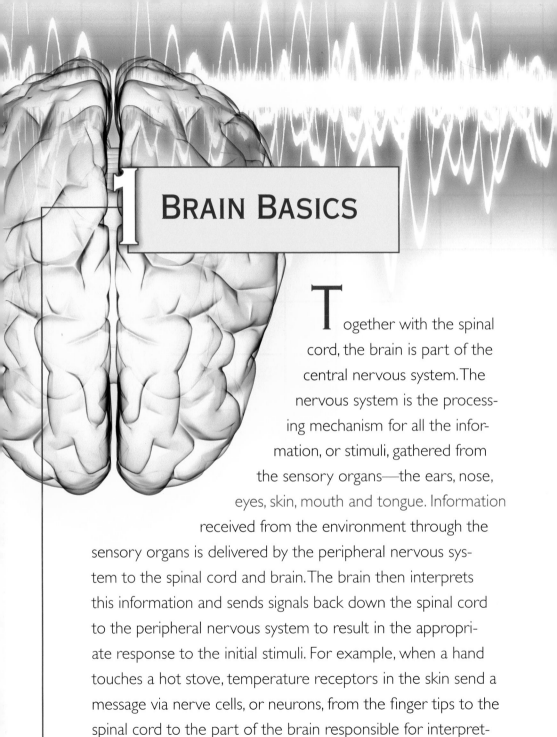

1 BRAIN BASICS

Together with the spinal cord, the brain is part of the central nervous system. The nervous system is the processing mechanism for all the information, or stimuli, gathered from the sensory organs—the ears, nose, eyes, skin, mouth and tongue. Information received from the environment through the sensory organs is delivered by the peripheral nervous system to the spinal cord and brain. The brain then interprets this information and sends signals back down the spinal cord to the peripheral nervous system to result in the appropriate response to the initial stimuli. For example, when a hand touches a hot stove, temperature receptors in the skin send a message via nerve cells, or neurons, from the finger tips to the spinal cord to the part of the brain responsible for interpreting types of touch sensation. The brain interprets the signal and

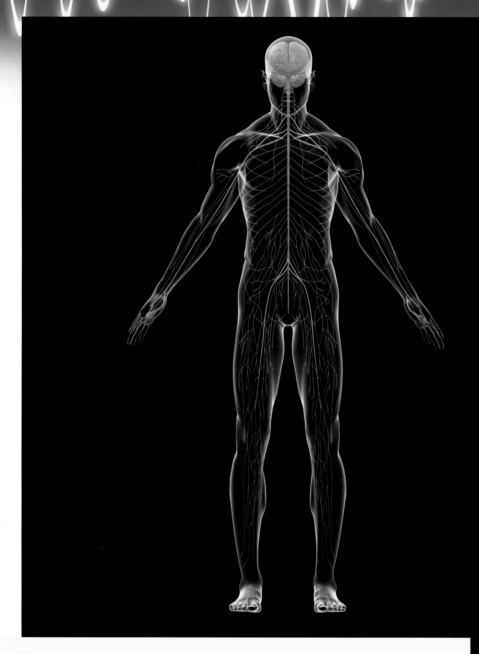

Like a network of electrical wires, the nervous system consists of major nerve pathways that divide into smaller and smaller branches, some responsible for movement, others for sensation.

immediately sends an outgoing nerve impulse to the peripheral nervous system and the motor muscles of the hand with a message telling the person that the stove is hot. This leads to the withdrawal of the hand from the hot stove. Because of the unique structure of neurons, all of this takes place in seconds.

Cerebral Cortex

The human brain looks like a large pinkish-grey, fleshy walnut. This outermost area of the brain is called the cerebral cortex. The cerebral cortex is responsible for most of the human brain's higher functioning—that is, memory, awareness, thought, and even consciousness. The brain's cortex is intricately folded, resulting in gyri (bumps) and sulci (grooves). These folds increase the surface area of the brain. The greater the surface area, the more room for neural activity. Without folding, the human brain would be roughly the size of a full newspaper page and would never fit inside the skull. While no two human brains have the exact same folding pattern, the basic structure of individual human brains is the same.

The Two Hemispheres

The cerebral cortex can be divided right down the middle into two identical halves, or hemispheres. In most people, the left hemisphere controls the right side of the body and the right hemisphere controls the left side of the body. The evolutionary reason for this crossover of motor and sensory function is unclear.

The two hemispheres of the brain generally have specific functions. In most people, the left hemisphere is more involved in language, math, logic, abstract reasoning, and the use of and interpretation of symbols. The right hemisphere tends to have more of a role in understanding the space around us, interpretation of information from the senses, recognizing faces, and artistic endeavors such as playing music or painting. The two hemispheres do communicate and are connected by the corpus callosum, a thick band of 200 to 250 million nerve fibers.

Four Lobes of the Brain

The two hemispheres of the brain can be divided further into four lobes. The frontal lobes are involved in thinking and reasoning, memory, concentration, and learning. They also play a role in controlling voluntary motor activity, such as choosing to pick something up off the floor, personality, emotional behavior, judgment and inhibition of behavior, and translating thought to words. When someone becomes very angry and has an impulse to scream or hit something, the frontal lobes help inhibit, or suppress, this behavior. The frontal lobes also enable the planning of a schedule over time and imagination of future events. The frontal lobes are

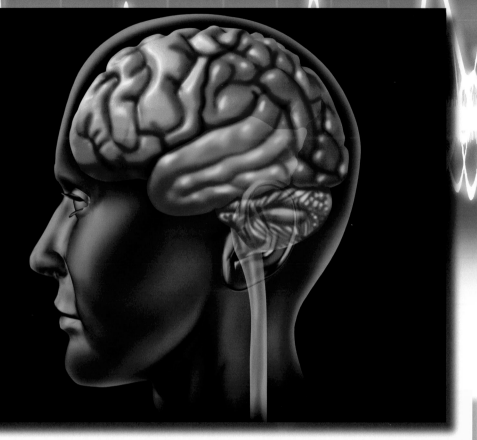

The brain can be divided into functional areas. The orange, pink, purple, and green areas represent the frontal, parietal, occipital, and temporal lobes, respectively. The textured pink is the cerebellum.

thought to act as a short-term storage site for ideas; while there is the consideration of one idea, others are kept in mind at the same time.

The parietal lobes help process sensory information including touch, temperature, pressure, taste, and pain from the entire body. They are also involved in helping appropriately orient the body in space based on the perception and recognition of information received by the senses.

The temporal lobes are involved in perception and recognition of auditory information from the ears, including interpreting frequency, pitch, and location of sound in space. The temporal lobes also include an important structure called the hippocampus, a brain region crucial to the formation and recollection of long-term memories.

The hippocampal areas within the temporal lobes are also needed for spatial memory, or to remember how to navigate through spaces one has been in before. It is thought to be responsible for the "cognitive map" humans use to remember where we've been and to get where we are going. The hippocampus is an important structure within the temporal lobes of the brain that is crucial in the development of new memories and spatial navigation based on memory.

The occipital lobes receive and process visual information from the eyes and relay it to other areas of the brain. They are important in the recognition and identification of objects and patterns using images stored in memory. For example, this is how someone is able to recognize a pen each time he or she picks it up instead of having to be told what it is. Reading the words on this page also requires the use of the occipital lobes to link the words with associated images stored in memory.

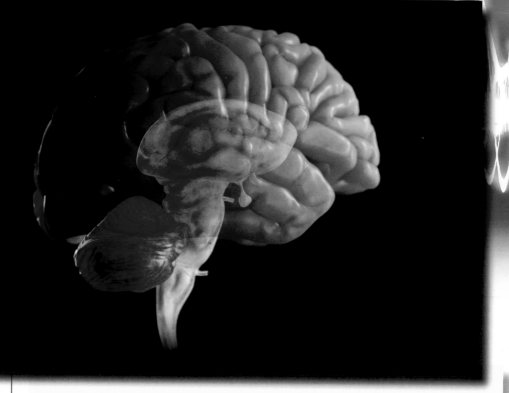

The brain stem attaches directly to the spinal cord and acts as a relay station; all communication between the brain and the body travels through the brain stem.

The Brain Stem

The brain stem is a deep and primitive part of the brain that is located just above the top of the spinal cord and serves as the gateway between the brain and the rest of the organs of the body. The structures of the brain stem (the medulla, pons, and midbrain) are responsible for functions crucial to basic life, such as breathing, maintaining heart rate and blood pressure, reflexes, digestion, sweating, and vestibular function

The Cerebellum: "Little Brain"

The cerebellum is a cauliflower-shaped part of the brain that helps coordinate and appropriately time voluntary movement in terms of balance and coordination of muscles. It is located at the lower back part of the brain near the brain stem. Voluntary movements include actions such as walking, talking, chewing, swallowing, dancing, jogging, or swinging a baseball bat. The cerebellum is also involved with posture and enables precision movement. It allows these actions to occur without much thought, acting as an autopilot. New studies also suggest that the cerebellum may also be involved in attention, language, and mental imagery.

(balance). It is also involved in the level of alertness, or consciousness.

Cranial Nerves

The brain stem is the origin of the twelve pairs of cranial nerves. Some of these nerves bring information from the sensory organs to the brain and are involved in vision, taste, smell, and hearing, while others control facial movement and sensation, swallowing reflexes, eye movements, and the ability to shrug the shoulders. Cranial nerve I is involved in smell. Cranial nerve II transmits visual information from the eyes to the occipital lobe for interpretation. Cranial nerve III controls most movements of the eye and allows the pupil to constrict to control the amount of light entering the eye. Cranial nerve IV is also involved with certain eye movements. Cranial nerve V is involved in facial sensation and the muscles of chewing. Cranial nerve VI is also involved in specific eye movement. Cranial nerve VII is involved in taste, salivation, eye tearing, and muscles of facial expression. Cranial nerve VIII is involved in hearing and balance. Cranial nerve IX controls taste, salivation, and muscles of swallowing. Cranial nerve X aids in swallowing, voice, heart rate control, and actions of the lungs, digestive organs, and bladder. Cranial nerve XI helps control shrugging and head movement. Cranial nerve XII controls movement to part of the tongue and is involved in speech and swallowing.

Wernicke's and Broca's Areas

Wernicke's area is located on the left side of the brain where the parietal and temporal lobes meet. This region functions in understanding auditory and visual information, associating sights and sound with memory, and giving meaning to memory. Wernicke's area is also involved in understanding spoken and written language. Another specialized region, Broca's area, is located near the left frontal-parietal junction and helps turn internal concepts and ideas into spoken words.

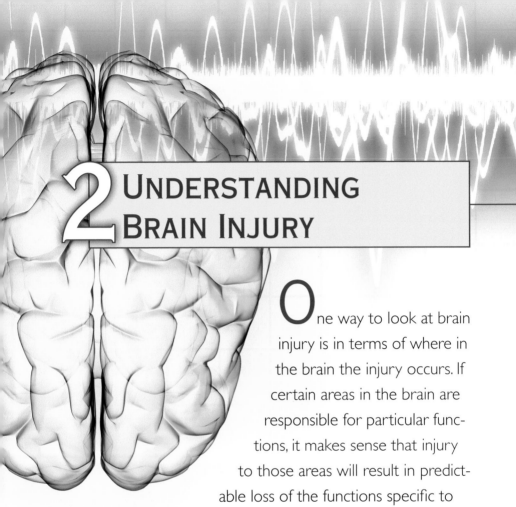

2 UNDERSTANDING BRAIN INJURY

One way to look at brain injury is in terms of where in the brain the injury occurs. If certain areas in the brain are responsible for particular functions, it makes sense that injury to those areas will result in predictable loss of the functions specific to those brain regions, in whole or in part. By observing changes in behavior and loss or impairment of specific functions in people who have suffered an injury to particular parts of the brain, scientists can learn more about what those parts of the brain do.

Injury to a Hemisphere

Significant damage to one side of the brain or the other generally results in motor and sensory deficits of the opposite

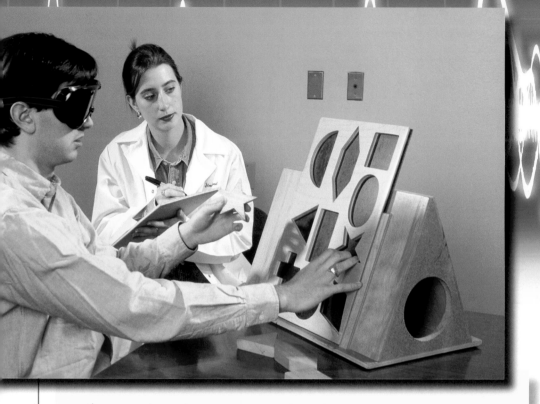

In a tactile performance test, a blindfolded patient matches blocks to spaces with the same shape, teaching a neurologist about her spatial memory and problem-solving ability.

side of the body. For example, when a person experiences an interruption of blood supply to the left side of the brain, he or she may have symptoms of weakness of the muscles or numbness and tingling and other sensory problems on the right side of the body. This is because the left side of the brain controls motor and sensation on the right side of the body.

In addition, because the right and left sides of the brain have some different functions, individuals with damage to the left side of the brain often have speech and language difficulties, whereas injury to the same region of the right side of the brain does not generally have these effects. Instead, injuries to the right hemisphere often cause problems more related to thinking and reasoning, organization, and problem solving.

Frontal Lobe Injury

Injury to one of the frontal lobes of the brain can result in motor and sensory deficits or paralysis on the opposite side of the body. However, it often has more behavioral effects such as difficulty concentrating and staying focused, behavior problems, difficulty learning new information and assigning meaning to words, lack of inhibition of inappropriate social behavior, loss of recent memory, and emotional disturbances.

Parietal Lobe Injury

Injury to one of the parietal lobes can result in disorientation in space, problems with hand-eye coordination, difficulty writing, inability to recognize or locate body parts, and inability to distinguish between types of sensory input (smell, sound, sight, taste).

Because of its involvement in coordination and spatial orientation, parietal lobe injury can cause apraxia, or difficulty remembering a sequence of movements required to complete a task. When most individuals get dressed, they do not need to

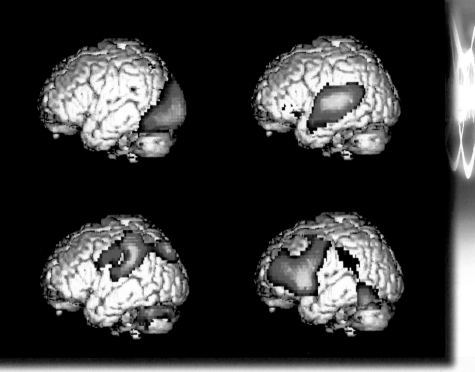

During a PET scan, the active areas of the brain light up. Changes from normal activity levels help neurologists determine what areas of the brain are damaged.

think about how to button their shirt—they just do it, without having to think of the steps involved. Some individuals with damage to the parietal lobe have to relearn how to button their shirts or tie their shoes.

Parietal lobe damage also can cause a specific type of agnosia, or an inability to recognize things by use of the senses. Such individuals may be unable to recognize and name everyday objects, such as a pencil or key, placed in the hand opposite the side of the brain that sustained injury.

Spatial Neglect Syndrome

Following brain injury due to stroke or bleeding in the brain, individuals may fail to clean, dress, or move one whole side of the body and even neglect one whole side of space (the left or right, depending on the site of brain injury). They may even deny that the limbs on the affected side belong to them. Spatial neglect syndrome can occur after strokes that involve the parietal lobes. Strokes or injury that involve the left parietal lobe can result in neglect of the right side of the body and the right side of space, and vice versa.

Temporal Lobe Injury

Imagine not being able to recognize familiar faces, such as that of loved ones or parents, despite seeing them every day and being able to recognize their voices or mannerisms. This is called prosopagnosia, a disorder of facial perception most commonly caused by damage to the fusiform gyrus, an area in the temporal lobe.

While some individuals are born with this disorder, it can be the result of trauma to the brain, as in the case of a twenty-four-year-old man studied by German neurologist Joachim Bodamer in 1947. This young man had been shot in the head and afterward was unable to recognize the faces of loved ones or his own face in the mirror without touching, listening to associated voices, or observing gait or mannerisms.

Temporal lobe injury can also result in an inability to recognize sounds or voices, including those of known individuals, even though hearing remains intact. Damage to the hippocampus within the temporal lobe can cause problems navigating a space by memory, such as a room in your house or roads you have driven on before, and it can cause problems with remembering new facts or events.

Dr. Oliver Sacks is a renowned neurologist, professor, and author. Not only does he study neurological conditions, he himself lives with prosopagnosia ("face blindness"), the inability to recognize faces, including his own.

Occipital Lobe Injury

Injury to the occipital lobes results in inability to read, hallucinations, difficulty identifying colors, and "visual field cuts" in both eyes. For example, individuals with an injury to the

10 GREAT QUESTIONS
TO ASK A NEUROLOGIST

1. What are the most common brain injuries?
2. What kind of treatment would I need after a head trauma?
3. What kind of imaging would I need after a head trauma: an MRI or CAT scan?
4. What kind of neurological tests will you perform if I have a brain injury?
5. What kinds of medicine for pain are safe to take?
6. What are the long-term side effects, if any, of brain injury?
7. What types of activity should I avoid to prevent brain injury?
8. Is a brain injury localized to a small part of the brain or a larger part?
9. What kind of complications may occur from concussion?
10. What symptoms of brain trauma should prompt me to seek medical care?

right side of the occipital lobe can lose the ability to process visual information sent from the left side of both eyes, while information from the right side of both eyes is seen normally.

Injury to the entire occipital lobe can result in total blindness, despite the fact that the eyes themselves are not injured and can technically "see." The eyes, however, are merely the location where we receive visual information. Without the occipital lobes to process and translate visual information, a person is functionally blind.

Brain Stem Injury

Because the brain stem is involved in control and regulation of basic life functions such as breathing, heart rate, digestion, and consciousness, injury to this very important brain area can be deadly. The brain stem can be injured itself or can be damaged incidentally as a result of downward pressure from swelling caused by injury to other areas of the brain. Brain stem injury can result in problems swallowing, the inability to breathe, cardiac arrest, paralysis, loss of consciousness, and even death as a result of complications from the loss of critical life functions.

Cranial Nerve Damage

Function and loss of function resulting from damage to the twelve pairs of cranial nerves can be tested easily without the

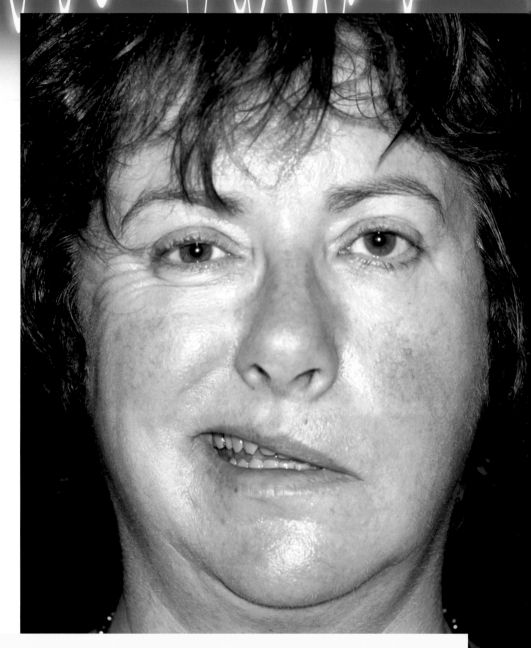

Bell's palsy is a type of facial paralysis caused by damage to cranial nerve VIII. It causes muscle weakness on one side of the face, as well as changes in saliva or tear production.

use of high-tech equipment. Since each nerve has a specific task, damage to these nerves results in the predictable loss of function. For example, people with damage to cranial nerve I cannot smell, a condition called anosmia. Damage to cranial nerve V can cause stabbing, electrical shocklike pain across the side of the face. Damage to cranial nerve VII, which controls facial muscles, can result in a very obvious drooping and inability to control the muscles on one side of the face, a condition commonly known as Bell's palsy.

Cerebellar Injury

Injury to the cerebellum results in slow, uncoordinated movements, instead of rapid, smooth movement. Individuals with damage to the cerebellum may have tremors, may walk with a sway or swagger (ataxia), may be unable to perform rapidly alternating movements such as moving the index finger between the nose and a moving target, and may have irregular, jerky eye movements.

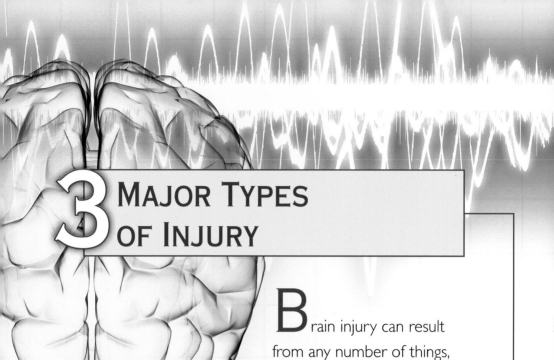

3 MAJOR TYPES OF INJURY

Brain injury can result from any number of things, some originating from outside the head, others from internal sources. Traumatic brain injury (TBI) occurs when the head is struck by, strikes, or is penetrated by something external to the body, such as a bullet, that disrupts the function of the brain. One of the most visible cases of TBI in recent memory was when congresswoman Gabrielle Giffords was shot in the head on January 8, 2011, in an apparent assassination attempt by Jared Lee Loughner. That she survived defied the odds, and Giffords, at the time of this writing, is recovering and rehabilitating remarkably well.

Recent data shows that there are 1.7 million TBIs in the United States every year. Many of these are fatal, but some are less severe. TBIs can be mild, resulting in a brief loss of

Democratic Representative Gabrielle Giffords suffered severe brain damage when she was shot in the head by a would-be assassin. Here she's pictured before (left) and after (right) the injury and partial rehabilitation.

consciousness or confusion, or severe, causing sustained loss of consciousness, memory loss, personality changes, or physical and mental disability.

Concussion

The most common cause of TBI is concussion, which results from a blow to the head from falling or from an object striking the head, or from a whiplash injury that causes the head to snap back and forth, as in a motor vehicle accident or

Hypoxia and Anoxia

Trauma to the brain can occur in cases where the brain tissue and cells are deprived of oxygen. This is called hypoxia when oxygen is low and anoxia when oxygen is absent completely. Without oxygen, cells cannot survive. This can occur in localized areas, as in the case of stroke, where blood flow may be blocked by a clot in a single vessel. Hypoxia can also be more widespread, as in the case of internal bleeding due to trauma or a ruptured vessel.

Hypoxia can also cause brain-wide damage, as in the case of problems that cause the heart to stop pumping or the lungs to stop working well. These situations result in blood that is not carrying enough oxygen going to the brain, or failure of blood to reach the brain at all due to the heart failing to drive it there. These causes of hypoxia have the potential to cause very serious and permanent damage quickly.

physical assault. The force of the blow or movement causes the brain, which sits in a substance called cerebral spinal fluid (CSF), to slosh forward and backward against the sides of the skull.

Concussions are typically mild injuries and are usually not life threatening. They are often sustained by athletes and are preventable with appropriate protection in the form of a good helmet. While people with concussions usually recover quickly, the symptoms and signs of concussion can last days to months. These can include vision changes, headache, nausea, vomiting, dizziness, drowsiness, behavior change such as irritability, difficulty concentrating, difficulty remembering new information, and light or noise sensitivity. Some symptoms occur right away, while others occur over several days.

Anyone with a suspected concussion, whether loss of consciousness occurs or not, should be seen by a medical professional to rule out a more serious brain injury, many of which have similar initial symptoms. Symptoms suggesting more severe injury are speech problems, severe headache, weakness or clumsiness, and continued vomiting. Treatment for concussion involves rest, avoidance of contact sports, and physical activity. New research indicates that activities that require lots of concentration can slow recovery, too.

The clear cerebral spinal fluid that encases the brain and circulates through the ventricles helps protect the brain from pressure and damage. Testing the fluid can help diagnose infections of the brain.

Helmet Technology and Trauma Prevention

The risk of traumatic brain injury can be reduced using common sense and some simple, everyday devices. Helmets should be worn when playing sports such as football, hockey, bicycling, skiing, and snowboarding. No matter what your level of skill—novice or near-professional—always wearing a helmet during such activities is your best chance of protecting yourself against potentially fatal head injuries. Most U.S. states and Canadian provinces have even made it the law for youths to wear a helmet while bicycling.

Recent studies revealed that most concussions during football games result from hits to the jaw and the side of the head and face, not the back or top of the head. For this reason, newer helmets have been designed that better protect these areas and are sized for individual users for a snugger, more protective fit. Many have inflatable pads inside and newer, harder shells to cushion blows to the head. Such helmets are being used not only in the National Football League (NFL), but also in high schools. Research suggests that using these helmets results in a 31 percent reduction of concussion in users. Other means of preventing traumatic brain injuries include using seat belts while in a car, not driving under the influence of alcohol or drugs, use of proper motorcycle and bike helmets, and safety education programs about driving laws.

Skull Fractures, Hematomas, and Hemorrhage

Direct trauma to the head can cause other types of severe injury. One injury that can occur is a skull fracture. While linear cracks in the bones of the skull may not result in brain injury, displaced or depressed skull fractures can be associated with broken bone fragments piercing or bruising the brain, causing serious damage. They can disrupt the function of the injured brain area, cause bleeding, and introduce bacteria and debris to the brain from the outside world. This can result in infection and further damage. A blow to the head can also cause bleeding inside the brain (hemorrhage). Quickly or over time, bleeding can cause compression of the brain tissue, permanent damage, and even death.

The brain is covered by three layers of membrane: the dura mater, the arachnoid mater, and the pia mater. Three types of brain bleeding can be described in terms of their relation to these layers. An epidural hematoma is a collection of blood between the skull and the dura mater, resulting from the rupture of high pressure and fast bleeding arteries. Subdural hematomas, or bleeding between the dura mater and the arachnoid mater, can also occur from blows to the head and typically result in the rupture of slower bleeding veins. Lastly, subarachnoid hemorrhages occur between the arachnoid and pia mater. These types of bleeds generally have the highest risk of death and progress quickly. Without immediate recognition and treatment, the

chance of death or perma-
nent damage is very high.

In many cases, individuals
with traumatic brain bleeds
have very obvious symptoms.
Unfortunately, some brain
bleeds (particularly epidural
hematomas) may not cause
serious symptoms at first, so
individuals may initially appear
fine. Only later do symptoms
develop, which can be life
threatening if unrecognized.

Sometimes, people do go
to the doctor, and because
they do not have severe
symptoms, they are assumed
to have a mild concussion
when in fact they are bleeding

Actress Natasha Richardson died of an epidural hematoma two days after she struck her head while skiing without a helmet. She declined medical evaluation because she claimed that she felt fine.

within the brain. This delay in diagnosis can be deadly. Even minor
blows to the head without loss of consciousness can result in
brain bleeds, though this is more likely in older adults, people with
underlying brain abnormalities, or people who are on medications
that make them more vulnerable to bleeding. For these reasons,
all blows to the head, even those with minor symptoms, should
be taken seriously by patients, their families, and medical providers.

MYTHS AND FACTS

Myth: Brain injury happens only to older people.

Fact: While certain types of brain injury are more likely in older people, brain injury can happen to people of any age.

Myth: If I hit my head hard but don't feel any dizziness or pain, I don't need to be seen by a doctor.

Fact: All head injuries should be checked out by a medical professional, whether a person is young or old, a helmet was worn or not, and even if a person feels fine right after. It is better to be safe than sorry.

Myth: I don't need to wear a helmet during sports like skiing, snowboarding, biking, football, and wrestling if I am really good at them.

Fact: Even if you are a skilled athlete, you should always wear a helmet during sports such as football, skiing, snowboarding, biking, and wrestling. Even skilled athletes sustain brain injuries, many of which can be prevented or made less severe with helmet use.

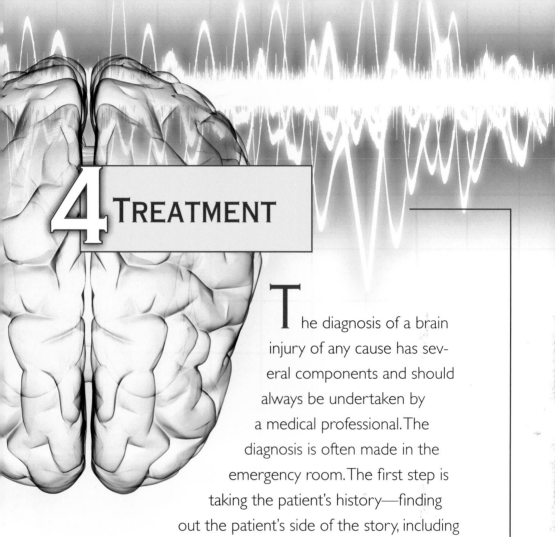

4 TREATMENT

The diagnosis of a brain injury of any cause has several components and should always be undertaken by a medical professional. The diagnosis is often made in the emergency room. The first step is taking the patient's history—finding out the patient's side of the story, including what happened and when, if he or she lost consciousness and for how long, if he or she wore a helmet if playing a sport, and what the patient's symptoms or complaints are. The doctor will ask if the person vomited; is having vision changes, weakness, tingling, or difficulty speaking; when the symptoms started; if they are worsening; and how severe they are.

Also important are questions about the patient's general health, family history, prescribed medications, and recreational drug or alcohol use. In cases of brain injury, family members

and friends often contribute to the history by reporting behavior changes, speech problems, drowsiness, or other signs of brain injury the patient himself or herself might not notice. The history is sometimes the most telling part of the exam, leading a medical provider to suspect brain injury, but diagnosis of brain injury cannot be made on this basis alone.

A medical provider tests a patient's reflexes. Changes in response from the norm can indicate a problem with the peripheral or central nervous system, including brain or spinal cord injury.

Physical Exam

A physical exam is the next step and generally involves simple tests that look for neurological deficits or loss of function. The medical provider will test the patient's movement, sensation, strength, and reflexes to be sure they are present and equal in all limbs. The patient's level of awareness and alertness will be evaluated. The patient's pupils will be checked and compared for responsiveness to light and size.

Other cranial nerves will be checked for symmetry on either side of the face, speech problems, eye muscle problems, and vision changes. The patient's head, neck, and face will be evaluated for signs of obvious trauma, including bruises, deformities, depressions in the bone, bleeding inside the ears, cracking sounds with pressure, and deep cuts. Heart rate, breathing rate, temperature, and oxygen levels will be checked for abnormalities.

Imaging and Recording the Brain

The findings on the physical exam, coupled with the history, can give a doctor a clue to whether a brain injury occurred and what type. A more definitive diagnosis of brain injury is best made by taking pictures of the brain or by measuring its electrical activity. This can be done in several ways, none of which are painful or invasive. A computed tomography (CT) scan uses radiation to take pictures of the brain in thin cross sections with high detail. These images are then digitally put together to create a three-dimensional picture of the brain that can be examined by a radiologist for abnormalities. This is similar to placing a sliced loaf of bread on a counter and taking the slices away, one after the next, beginning at one end. Each removed slice allows a deeper glimpse into the bread loaf to see contours that cannot be seen from the outside. CT scans can be useful in diagnosing new bleeding in the

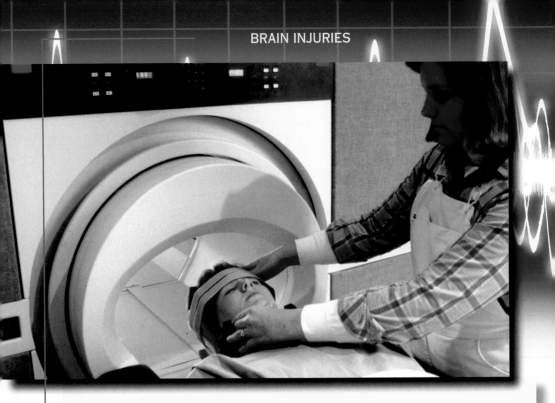

A woman is about to undergo an MRI of her brain to check for abnormalities. A painless procedure, an MRI requires the patient to be very still. To help, soft head restraints are often used.

brain, wasting away of brain tissue, skull fractures, and some brain tumors.

An MRI, or magnetic resonance imaging scan, is another way to see inside the brain and look for abnormalities. Instead of X-rays, MRIs use radio frequency pulses and a powerful magnetic field to create this three-dimensional image. MRIs are better suited to see old injuries, observe healing over time, and look for soft tissue masses, such as tumors, whereas CT scans are used to look for acute injuries, new bleeding, and skull fractures. CT scans are usually more readily available in emergency room settings and are much faster to perform. Special types of MRI, however, can also be used to observe brain function. MRAs, or magnetic resonance angiograms, are special tests that can be used to look specifically at the vessels that supply blood to the brain and to look for areas of blockage or rupture. CT scans or MRIs of the brain after the injection of a special dye into the veins can highlight infectious abscesses and changes to the myelin sheaths surrounding neurons in cases of some neurological diseases.

An EEG, or electroencephalogram, measures the electrical activity of the brain using electrodes attached to the scalp on one end and a computer on the other. This study produces wave patterns that can be read to determine if the neurons of the brain are functioning properly. An EEG is useful to determine if a person in a coma has underlying activity or if he or she is brain dead; to evaluate the full extent of damage caused by Alzheimer's disease or other causes of dementia; to diagnose seizure disorders, neurological diseases, and mental health issues; and to study sleep disorders. EEGs may also be used to observe the brain for changes in function during brain surgery procedures.

A PET scan, or positron emission tomography, relies on the brain's natural use of glucose for energy. The patient receives glucose "tagged" with a radioactive molecule that can be tracked as it moves through the brain. Areas of the brain with damage use less energy and will show less of the

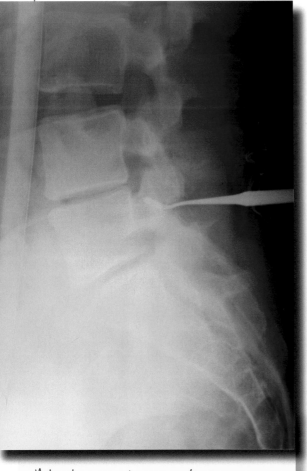

A lumbar puncture can diagnose infections, bleeding, or inflammation in the central nervous system. It must be performed under sterile conditions to prevent germs from entering the spinal fluid.

radioactive material than the rest of the brain.

Lumbar Puncture

A lumbar puncture, or "spinal tap," may be performed in cases where infection in the brain, such as meningitis or encephalitis, is suspected. A lumbar puncture involves inserting a needle between two vertebrae, the stacked bones of the spine, to collect and test the fluid that bathes the meninges of the spinal cord and brain. The fluid is sent to a laboratory for analysis under the microscope and culture for infections.

Blood Tests

A person with a suspected brain injury might have blood taken to look for signs of infection. Blood work can also tell a doctor if the person has lost a lot of blood and may need a blood transfusion to replace the blood lost. Special blood tests can also help diagnose some neurological conditions, as well as tell the doctors if the person has a problem with blood clotting— for example, if the blood forms clots too quickly or if it does not clot quickly enough.

Immediate and Long-term Treatments

Treatments for brain injury depend on the type of injury that occurs. Mild brain injuries like concussions generally require physical and mental rest (no sports, work, driving, or school until symptoms fade), medicine for headache, lots of fluids, and careful observation by family or friends for worsening symptoms that could indicate more serious brain trauma.

Most brain injuries other than mild concussions require the patient to stay in the hospital for observation and treatment. A patient may need to be sent to a hospital that specializes in brain injury. Many specialists may be involved in the patient's care, including neurologists, orthopedists who deal with bone fractures, psychiatrists, surgeons, and infectious disease doctors. The more rapidly a brain injury is diagnosed and treated, the better the chance of recovery. The goal is restoration of blood and oxygen flow to the brain and prevention of further damage or infection.

Treatment of mild bleeding inside the brain requires careful monitoring for worsening symptoms. More aggressive intervention may be necessary for significant bleeding and may require drainage of collected blood that can put too much pressure on the rest of the brain. Probes may be inserted through the skull and into the brain to detect pressure buildup that would require further drainage of blood through a temporary tube or even by removing a small piece of the skull to relieve pressure. Sometimes pieces of damaged brain are removed to allow more room for healthy tissue to thrive. Penetrating injuries to the brain, such as gunshot wounds, generally require surgery to stop bleeding, repair skull fractures, and remove debris stuck in the brain.

In the hospital, medicines may be given to keep the patient's blood pressure down, to draw extra fluid from the brain tissue, and to prevent seizure and infection. Often a person with severe brain injury is sedated and placed on machines to help him or her breathe while undergoing treatment for the injury. In some cases, the sedated patient may require additional medications to temporarily paralyze him or her. These machines also monitor the heart, blood pressure, and oxygen levels.

Recovery

At one time, scientists believed that the brain could not heal, like skin can, and that the number of brain cells we are born with are all we get. New research suggests otherwise and is

Exercising the Brain

Individuals who sustain a brain injury may suffer from memory loss, problems with concentration, inability to learn new things, difficulty expressing themselves with words or gestures, difficulty with activities requiring a sequence of actions (such as tying a shoe or buttoning a shirt), disorganization, and difficulty solving new problems, such as what to do if they get lost or injured. As part of rehabilitation both inside the hospital and out, people who have suffered a traumatic brain injury often undergo cognitive therapies that help them regain these lost functions. These "brain exercises" often involve daily puzzles, word games, memory tests, games that involve simple math, tossing and catching small objects from hand to hand or with another person, and even tasks involving drawing or sculpting objects out of clay.

promising in terms of our ability to recover from some types of brain injury. Scientists have found that new neurons do regenerate, through neurogenesis. Research also shows that some nerve cells of the brain have plasticity—that is, they can change their structure and function in response to injury or damage.

Individuals who sustain a mild brain injury generally recover over days to months with adequate rest alone. Those who suffer more serious brain injury requiring hospitalization or surgery often have a rougher and longer road ahead. This often

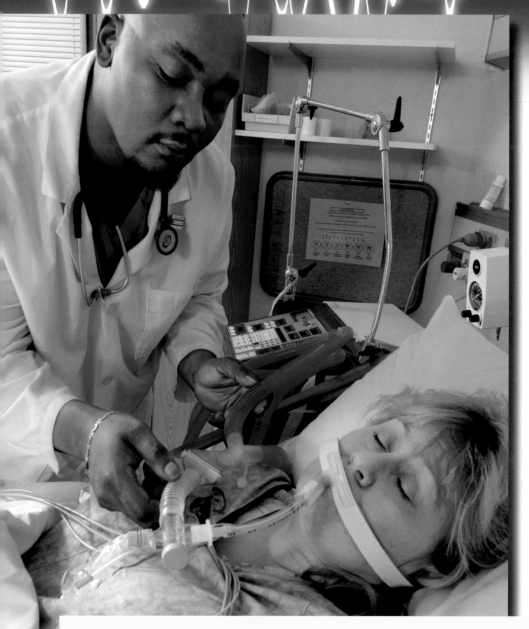

Patients with severe brain injury often require intubation and a ventilator to assist their breathing. They may also need machines to monitor heart rate, blood pressure, oxygen levels, and pressure around the brain.

includes rehabilitation services to help them recover motor and cognitive functions lost because of injury and possibly a longer stay in a hospital under sedation and on life-support machines. For example, a person who has suffered stroke may not only have weakness in the legs due to being bedridden while under treatment, but may also have difficulty moving one side or part of the body. Someone who had bleeding in the Broca's area, which controls motor for speech, may have to learn how to speak again.

Rehabilitation services involve daily therapy of several types, at first in a special facility, and then at home. A patient may be placed on a treadmill at slow speeds with support while relearning how to walk without falling, either on his or her own or with a cane or walker. Rehabilitation special-ists will make sure patients can perform their "activities of daily living" before going home. These include basic actions required to take care of oneself at home, like grooming (brushing teeth, showering), getting dressed, using stairs, get-ting up out of bed and from chairs, eating, using the bath-room, using the phone, cooking, doing housework, and man-aging paperwork and finances.

Novel Approaches to Treatment

Plasticity, or the ability of neurons to adapt to damage, as well as the discovery that the brain does produce some new neurons through neurogenesis, has prompted researchers to look into what happens on a molecular level to trigger this adaptation and new growth in the hopes of developing new treatments to heal the brain more rapidly after injury. Scientists are currently trying to isolate the chemical substances, or growth factors, that might trigger and direct such activity. One group of researchers is experimenting with an injectable gel that contains chemicals that stimulate cell growth and development. This substance would be injected into the wound site. Other research involves the injection of healthy brain cells donated from other people. This has not been a promising line of study, since it seems the cells may not get enough blood or nutrients because of swelling at the injury site.

The discovery of stem cells, unprogrammed cells that have the ability to become specialized cell types with the right chemical triggers, may be useful in the treatment of brain injury if scientists are able to deliver these special cells to the right areas of the brain and discover the growth factors that would cause them to develop into the kind of neurons that are needed in a particular area of the brain. One group of researchers is exploring taking bone marrow stem cells from children with traumatic brain injuries and injecting them into the injured part of their brains. Thus far, it is unclear if the procedure is effective, but initial studies suggest no further damage is caused. Neural stem cells have also been discovered, and scientists are looking to them as a way

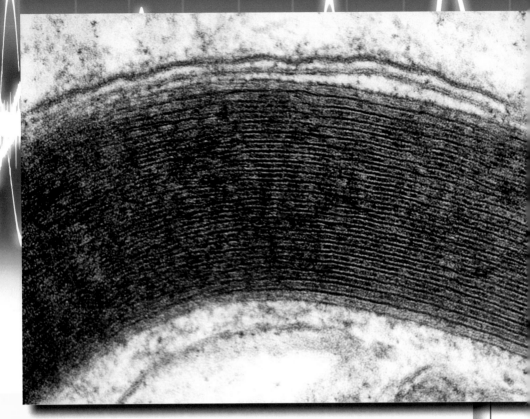

The myelin sheath insulating some nerves allows electrical impulses to move rapidly down the axon. Some neurological conditions cause a breakdown of myelin, resulting in decreased transmission of nerve signals.

of producing myelin, the sheathing along axons that allows for more rapid transmission of nerve impulses. These cells could be used in the treatment of damage caused by various neurological disorders.

Scientists have also been experimenting with injecting gene therapy as a means of treating brain injury caused by trauma, tumors, or neurological disease. Gene therapy involves the delivery of genes that code for specific proteins or substances to the site of brain injury, tumor, or disease in hopes that the cells of the surrounding tissue will pick them up, integrate them into their own DNA, and begin producing the proteins they code for. For example, in the case of cancerous brain tumors, scientists are working on delivering a gene that codes for a toxin that interferes with tumor growth. If the gene can be successfully taken up by the cells of the tumor or the surrounding healthy brain tissue, and if they begin to produce the toxin the gene codes for, the tumor may begin to shrink and die. Gene therapy may also be useful in cases where brain tissue has been damaged due to trauma or stroke. If genes for substances that trigger new neuron growth can be isolated and appropriately delivered, researchers may be able to stimulate the regrowth of brain tissue.

Other research suggests that when brain cells undergo trauma, a large amount of the ion calcium rushes into the axons of the nerve cells and may result in axon swelling that can cause the detachment of the axon from the rest of the nerve cell. In addition, this calcium influx also triggers the release of chemicals that break down damaged cells. The problem is that this onslaught of chemicals in response to cell damage can damage nearby cells that were not injured initially, causing the loss of more neurons. Scientists are looking at medicines that might slow or control this calcium influx in response to injury to protect axon damage.

Another promising field of research involves attempting to slow brain cell damage and death after traumatic brain injury using hypothermia, or cooling the injured person's body below its usual 98.6 degrees Fahrenheit (37 degrees Celsius), within eight hours of the injury. Patients under forty-five years of age with traumatic brain injury who were cooled to 91.4 °F (33 °C) seem to have fared better than those who were not cooled.

While many of these new techniques have shown promise in animal and human testing, much research is still in its early stages. Scientists have to make very sure an experiment not only works to achieve the desired goal, but that it is also safe for the patient. For this reason, experiments are first carried out on animal species.

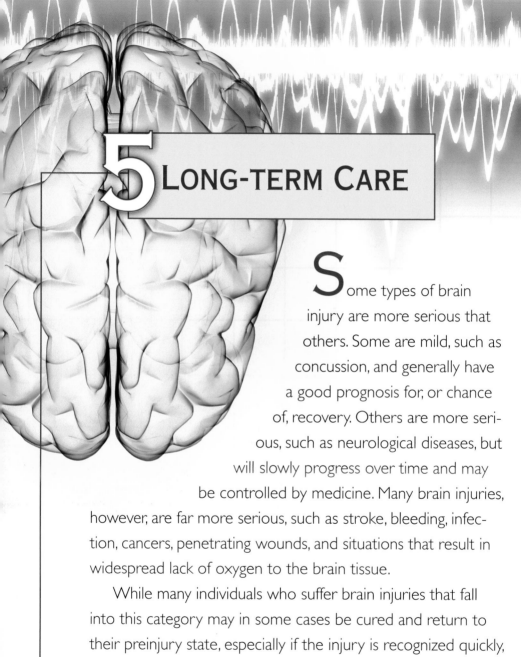

5 LONG-TERM CARE

Some types of brain injury are more serious that others. Some are mild, such as concussion, and generally have a good prognosis for, or chance of, recovery. Others are more serious, such as neurological diseases, but will slowly progress over time and may be controlled by medicine. Many brain injuries, however, are far more serious, such as stroke, bleeding, infection, cancers, penetrating wounds, and situations that result in widespread lack of oxygen to the brain tissue.

While many individuals who suffer brain injuries that fall into this category may in some cases be cured and return to their preinjury state, especially if the injury is recognized quickly, many of these serious injuries have long-term effects beyond weakness, speech problems, or other isolated neurological problems. Some of them will die as a result of brain injury, due to blood loss or loss of all function. Others, however, may fall into a coma or even a persistent vegetative state.

Severe injury to parts of the brain, usually the cerebral cortex, can result in coma, a deep unconscious state during which an individual cannot consciously respond to the outside environment. Individuals in a coma are not simply asleep and cannot be roused by shaking, bright lights, yelling, or even pain. They do not react to the voices of loved ones. The brain wave patterns, or electrical activity of the brains, of people in comas are markedly different than those of people that are asleep. These brain

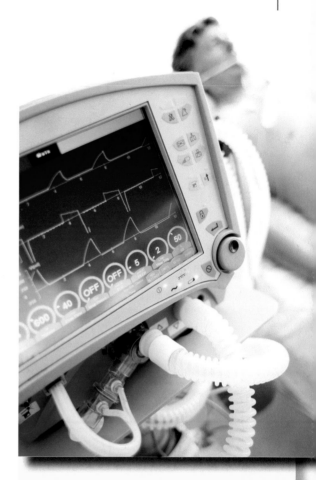

Severe brain injuries can result in coma, in which the patient must rely on equipment to monitor functions such as heart and breathing rates.

wave patterns, measured by EEGs, can help tell medical providers where the brain is damaged and how severe it is. If lower areas of the brain, such as the brain stem, are damaged, the

49

comatose individual may need a machine called a ventilator to help him or her breathe and a feeding tube to help him or her get nutrition.

Patients may require the insertion of a tube into the skull and brain to relieve pressure caused by trauma. Tubes may be placed into the bladder to help the patient urinate. If the cause of coma is related to drug or alcohol use, infection, epilepsy, too much or too little sugar in the blood, or liver problems, medications may be given to reverse the effects of these conditions. Nurses will turn the patient regularly to check for bed sores that can result from constant pressure on the buttocks and other pressure points from being still for so long. A physical therapist will visit daily to move the patient's arms and legs in order to prevent the muscles from atrophying, or wasting away. Blood work, urine samples, and chest X-rays may be regularly checked to monitor for infection or organ failure. Neurological exams will be routinely performed, as will evaluations of level of consciousness.

Comas generally last days to weeks, but they can last months to years. Recovery depends on the kind, duration, and severity of the brain injury; whether it was quickly recognized and easily reversible; the appropriate medical intervention and subsequent care; and the brain's ability to heal. On waking, one person may regain full mental and physical functioning, whereas another might require years of physical therapy and still not regain 100 percent of previous abilities. In the worst-case

The Glasgow Coma Scale

Scientists have developed a tool to help measure the depth of a coma or a person's level of consciousness by observing eye opening, speech, and movement. In the deepest stages of coma, a person will not open the eyes, speak, or move at all in response to anything. This is a Glasgow Coma Scale score of 3, the lowest score attainable. Fully conscious patients will spontaneously open their eyes; are oriented to where they are, who they are, and what the date is; and will move parts of their body when asked to do so. The GSC is not used to diagnose coma, but it is useful as part of an initial exam, when the person comes into the hospital, to assess and follow mental status. It is also useful for monitoring worsening or improvement over time.

scenario, some individuals regain only very basic bodily functions and may never be able to live an unassisted life. The longer a person is in a coma, generally speaking, the less likely the chance of full recovery.

Vegetative States

Those who do not recover from coma may be considered to be in a persistent vegetative state (PVS), generally as a result of widespread damage from which the brain cannot recover. While this can occur in the absence of initial coma, it often occurs when individuals in a coma recover some brain stem function—such as control of heart rate, blood pressure, and reflexes—but still have no activity in the cerebral cortex, which is responsible for higher functions such as consciousness, communication, thinking, and reasoning. People in a PVS may appear to respond to their surroundings. They may startle due to loud noise, blink, chew, swallow, make some noises, or grasp things in their hands, and their eyes may slowly wander as if they are purposefully looking at something. They may appear to smile or frown. These activities can give desperate family members false hope of improvement or recovery. Still, a person in a vegetative state will not follow commands to move, blink, or speak. When this situation lasts longer than a month, it is considered a PVS.

Palliative Care

An approach called palliative care has become a wonderful option for those with little or no chance of recovery. It allows them to live and, eventually, to die with dignity and in comfort when that time comes. The primary goal of palliative care is not to provide a cure but to assure quality of life in situations where there may be no cure. It acknowledges the fact that some medical conditions are incurable and that the best treatment is sometimes simply managing pain, providing emotional and spiritual support, and avoiding unnecessary invasive medical

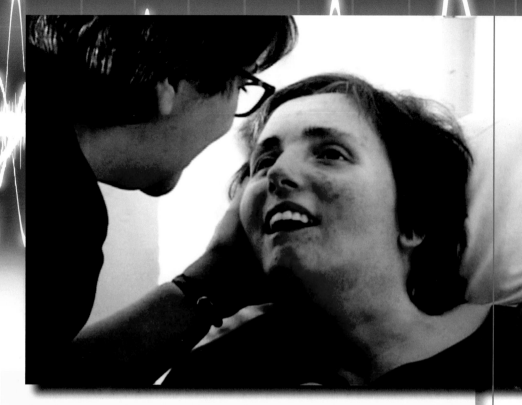

In 1990, Terri Schiavo collapsed. She wound up in a persistent vegetative state (PVS) due to oxygen deprivation. Her case incited debates about living wills, end-of-life decisions, and palliative care.

treatments and procedures that may only cause more suffering or prolong a chronic state. Palliative care also provides support for those who are still undergoing medical treatments that may be difficult and exhausting and that can result in depression and anxiety. The approach is highly respectful of an individual's unique needs, desires, and beliefs.

Palliative care generally involves a team of individuals whose only goal is to maintain the best quality of life possible. The person may be actively dying, have an incurable condition for which no treatment is available and from which they are not yet dying but may be suffering, or have a condition that is curable but requires taxing and sometimes painful treatment that may result in emotional distress. The team can involve doctors, nurses, spiritual counselors, massage therapists, nutritionists, cognitive therapists, pharmacists, and social workers, all of whom will collaborate to provide a person with care and help him or her make decisions that are for the best. The palliative care team also works with the families of the chronically ill to help them cope and to understand their loved one's needs and wishes. After a person who is chronically ill eventually passes away, the palliative care team will provide support for the family he or she has left behind, including coping with grief.

Glossary

aphasia The loss of the ability to speak or understand spoken or written language due to disease or injury of the brain.

axon A long fiber off a nerve cell that transmits information to other nerves or target organs.

Broca's area An area of the left frontal-parietal lobe associated with the motor control of speech.

central nervous system Part of the nervous system that consists of the brain and spinal cord.

cerebral cortex The highly folded outer surface of the brain responsible for higher brain functions, such as language and information processing.

coma A state of unconsciousness lasting several hours to several months in which a person cannot be awakened; cannot respond to painful stimuli, light, or sound; lacks a normal sleep-wake cycle; and does not initiate voluntary actions.

concussion A trauma-induced change in mental status that can cause confusion, amnesia, vomiting, and possible brief loss of consciousness.

corpus callosum The thick bridge of nervous tissue that connects the two hemispheres of the brain.

dendrite Branchlike projections off a nerve cell that receive information from other nerve cells or the surrounding environment.

embolus An abnormal particle, such as an air bubble, fat particle, or blood clot, circulating in the blood that can get stuck in small vessels and cut off blood supply.

hematoma A localized swelling due to the collection of blood, often due to the rupture of a blood vessel.

hemorrhage An excessive and rapid escape of blood from a vessel or vessels.

myelin The insulating material that surrounds nerve axons and facilitates the transmission of nerve impulses.

neuroscience The study of the human nervous system, including the brain and spinal cord, and the biological basis of consciousness, perception, memory, and learning.

palliative care An approach to health care that focuses primarily on attending to physical and emotional comfort, rather than effecting a cure for illnesses or conditions from which an individual is not likely to recover.

persistent vegetative state (PVS) A condition of profound unresponsiveness in a wakeful state caused by severe and permanent brain damage and characterized by a nonfunctioning cerebral cortex; absence of response to the external environment; and inability to signal, speak, or voluntarily move the body.

stroke An interruption of the blood supply to any part of the brain due to blockage or rupture of a vessel.

thrombus A blood clot formed in a blood vessel.

Wernicke's area An area of the brain that plays an important role in the comprehension of language.

For More Information

Brain Injury Association of America (BIAA)

1608 Spring Hill Road, Suite 110

Vienna, VA 22182

(703) 761-0750

Web site: http://www.biausa.org

The BIAA is the country's oldest and largest nationwide brain injury advocacy organization. Through advocacy, education and research, it brings help
to individuals living with brain injury, their families, and the professionals
who serve them.

Brain Injury Association of Canada (BIAC)

155 Queen Street, Suite 808

Ottawa, ON K1P 6L1

Canada

(866) 977-2492

Web site: http://www.biac-aclc.ca

This group aims to improve the quality of life for all Canadians affected by
acquired brain injury and promote its prevention. It's dedicated to facilitate
post-trauma research, education, and advocacy in partnership with national,
provincial/territorial, and regional associations and other stakeholders.

Centers for Disease Control and Prevention (CDC)

1600 Clifton Road

Atlanta, GA 30333

(800) 232-4636

Web site: http://www.cdc.gov

The CDC's mission is to create the expertise, information, and tools that
people and communities need to protect their health—through health

promotion; prevention of disease, injury, and disability; and preparedness for new health threats.

The Dana Foundation and the Dana Alliance for Brain Initiatives

745 Fifth Avenue, Suite 900

New York, NY 10151

(212) 223-4040

Web site: http://www.dana.org

This group is a private philanthropic organization that supports brain research through grants and educates the public about the successes and potential of brain research. It produces free publications, coordinates the International Brain Awareness Week campaign, and supports the Dana Alliances, a network of neuroscientists.

Mount Sinai Medical Center Palliative Care Program

One Gustave L. Levy Place

New York, NY 10029-6574

Web site: http://www.mountsinai.org/patient-care/service-areas/
palliative-care

(800) 637-4624

This program helps patients with advanced illnesses and their families make informed decisions regarding their health care when curative measures are no longer effective.

National Institute of Neurological Disorders and Stroke (NINDS)

P.O. Box 5801

Bethesda, MD 20824

(800) 352-9424

Web site: http://www.ninds.nih.gov

The mission of NINDS is to reduce the burden of neurological disease.

Web Sites

Due to the changing nature of Internet links, Rosen Publishing has developed an online list of Web sites related to the subject of this book. This site is updated regularly. Please use this link to access the list:

http://www.rosenlinks.com/bdis/binj

For Further Reading

Bradley, Walter George. *Treating the Brain: What the Best Doctors Know*. New York, NY: Dana Press, 2009.

Caplan, Louis R. *Stroke*. Saint Paul, MN: American Academy of Neurology, 2006.

Carter, Rita. *The Human Brain Book*. New York, NY: DK, 2009

Cassidy, John W. *Mindstorms: Living with Traumatic Brain Injury*. Cambridge, MA: Da Capo Lifelong Books, 2009.

Cleveland, Donald. *How Do We Know How the Brain Works*. New York, NY: Rosen Publishing, 2005.

Dolan, Carolyn E. *Brain Injury Rewiring for Survivors: A Lifeline to New Connections*. Enumclaw, WA: Idyll Arbor, 2010.

Gibbs, David. *Fighting for Dear Life. The Untold Story of Terri Schiavo and What It Means for All of Us*. Minneapolis, MN: Bethany House, 2006.

Gosling, Geo. *TBI Hell: A Traumatic Brain Injury Really Sucks*. Outskirt Press, 2006.

Mace, Nancy L. *The 36-hour Day: A Family Guide to Caring for People with Alzheimer Disease*. 4th ed. Baltimore, MD: Johns Hopkins University Press, 2006.

Marcovitz, Hal. *Brain Trauma*. Detroit, MI: Lucent Books, 2009.

Newquist, H. P. *The Great Brain Book: An Inside Look at the Inside of Your Head*. New York, NY: Scholastic Reference, 2005.

Nowinski, Christopher. *Head Games: Football's Concussion Crisis from the NFL to Youth Leagues*. East Bridgewater, MA: Drummond Publishing Group, 2007.

Senelick, Richard C. *Living with Stroke: A Guide for Families.* Birmingham, AL: HealthSouth Press, 2010.

Siles, Madonna. *Brain, Heal Thyself: A Caregiver's New Approach to Recovery from Stroke, Aneurysm, and Traumatic Brain Injury.* Charlottesville, VA: Hampton Roads, 2006.

Turkington, Carol. *The Encyclopedia of the Brain and Brain Disorders.* New York, NY: Facts On File, 2008.

Wilson, Michael R. *Frequently Asked Questions About How the Teen Brain Works.* New York, NY: Rosen Publishing, 2010.

Index

About the Author

Aubrey Stimola, M.P.A.S., graduated from Bard College, where she majored in bioethics, an academic blend of biology and philosophy, two branches of study that she feels are inseparable. She went on to work for a nonprofit public health organization in Manhattan, where she translated technical science and medical information into language comprehensible to a nonmedical audience. Her publications were designed to separate medical fact from fiction, the latter of which is dangerous and still abundant in the mainstream media and on the Internet. She performed a similar task for the New York State Department of Health before obtaining a master's degree in physician assistant sciences from Albany Medical College. Currently, she practices emergency medicine in Saratoga Springs, New York, as a physician assistant. She continues to enjoy writing medical nonfiction for a broad audience of readers.

Photo Credits

Cover (brain), pp. 7, 10 Shutterstock.com; p. 12 Science Picture Co./Science Faction/Getty Images; p. 16 Richard T. Nowitz/Photo Researchers; p. 18 © SPL/Custom Medical Stock Photo; p. 20 Chris McGrath/Getty Images News/Getty Images; p. 23 Dr. P. Marazzi/Photo Researchers; p. 26 © AP Images; p. 28 © F. D. Giddings/Phototake; p. 31 Dave M. Benett/Getty Images Entertainment/Getty Images; p. 34 Will & Deni McIntyre/Photo Researchers; p. 36 National Cancer Institute; p. 38 Ted Kinsman/Photo Researchers; p. 42 David Joel/Photographer's Choice/Getty Images; p. 45 David Phillips/Visuals Unlimited; p. 49 Science Photo Library/Getty Images; p. 53 Reuters/Ho/Landov; cover, back cover, and interior background images and elements (nerve cells, brain waves, brains) Shutterstock.com.

Designer: Les Kanturek; Editor: Nicholas Croce;
Photo Researcher: Marty Levick